The Newborn Pony

Do you love ponies? Be a Pony Pal!

The Newborn Pony

Jeanne Betancourt

illustrated by Paul Bachem

A
LITTLE APPLE
PAPERBACK

SCHOLASTIC INC.
New York   Toronto   London   Auckland   Sydney
Mexico City   New Delhi   Hong Kong

For Terry Icuso, a wise woman.

Thank you to Dr. Kent Kay and
Dr. Jayme Motler for their help in
preparing this manuscript.

ISBN 0-439-16571-7

12 11 10 9 8 7 6 5 4   2 3 4 5/0

Printed in the U.S.A.   40
First Scholastic printing, November 2000

Contents

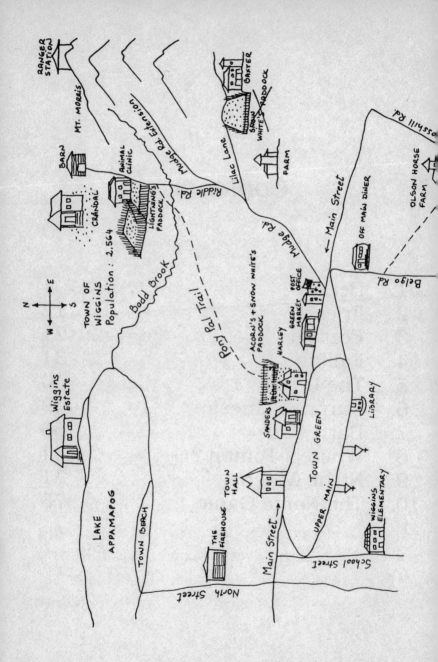

Beauty

The Pony Pals were tacked up with a tent, sleeping bags, and supplies. They were headed for a favorite Pony Pal campsite. It was in the hills behind Ms. Wiggins's house. Ms. Wiggins had a big property with a lot of great riding trails.

Lulu and her pony, Snow White, led the way along the trail. Lulu listened to the *clip-clop* of her friends' ponies behind her. Anna rode her Shetland pony, Acorn. Pam followed on her chestnut-colored pony, Lightning.

Lulu leaned forward and patted Snow

White's neck. "We're going to stop at Ms. Wiggins's and see your friend Beauty," she told her pony.

The trail widened. Now the three friends could ride side by side and talk.

"I wonder if Beauty had her foal last night," said Anna. "I'd love to see a newborn pony."

"I'd love to see a pony *being* born," said Lulu. "I've never seen that."

"I have," Pam told her friends. "It's amazing!"

"Maybe Beauty's having her foal today," said Anna. "Do you think Ms. Wiggins would let us stay and see it?"

"I bet she would," said Pam.

"I hope Mike Lacey isn't working for her today," said Anna.

Acorn snorted as if to say, "I don't like Mike Lacey."

The Pony Pals laughed. They didn't like Mike Lacey very much, either. Mike and his pal, Tommy Rand, were a few years older than the Pony Pals. Mike and Tommy liked

to tease the Pony Pals and play tricks on them. Sometimes the boys did stupid things that turned out to be dangerous. That's what Lulu disliked most about Tommy and Mike.

"Mike isn't so bad when he's not with Tommy," said Pam.

I still don't trust him, thought Lulu.

The trail narrowed. Again, there was only room for one pony at a time. Lulu moved back into the lead. The trail ahead of her was smooth and straight.

"Let's go, Snow White," Lulu told her pony.

Snow White made a happy snort as she moved into a smooth gallop. Lulu felt like she and Snow White were flying! It was a wonderful feeling.

When they reached the end of the trail, Lulu halted Snow White and waited for her friends.

The trail opened into a big field. Across the field Lulu saw Ms. Wiggins's paddocks, big house, and barn. Someone was in a paddock with Ms. Wiggins's horse, Picasso. Lulu couldn't tell who it was. She pulled the binoculars out of her pocket and looked through them. The person in the paddock was Mike Lacey.

Anna and Pam pulled their ponies alongside Lulu and Snow White.

"What are you looking at?" Pam asked Lulu.

"Mike," answered Lulu. She handed Pam the binoculars. "He's feeding Picasso."

"He put that feed bucket down in a hurry. Now he's running to the gate," said Pam. "I think Mike's afraid of Picasso."

"Look!" exclaimed Anna. "I can see him running out of the paddock. Did Picasso hurt him?"

"No," said Pam. "Picasso's busy eating."

"Besides," added Lulu, "Picasso would never hurt anyone. He's big, but he's sweet."

"Does Mike really look afraid?" asked Anna.

Pam handed Anna the binoculars. Anna peered through them. "You're right," she told Lulu. "He keeps looking over his shoulder to see if Picasso is following him."

"So Mike *is* working for Ms. Wiggins today," said Lulu with a sigh.

"Don't let him know where we're camping," warned Pam. "He might tell Tommy."

Anna was still using the binoculars. "Beauty's in the little paddock behind her stall," she told Lulu and Pam. "And she's still pregnant!"

The Pony Pals rode across the field. When they reached the barn they tied their ponies to the hitching post in front of it. Lulu didn't see Mike. Good, she thought. I hope he stays away from us.

Ms. Wiggins came out of the barn to greet the three girls. She was always happy to see the Pony Pals.

"You girls have great weather for a camping trip," she commented.

"How's Beauty?" asked Lulu.

"We stopped by to see her," added Pam.

"I think she'll have her foal very soon," said Ms. Wiggins.

The girls and Ms. Wiggins walked around to Beauty's little yard. When Beauty saw the

Pony Pals she came right over to them. Beauty's belly was big and round with the unborn foal.

Lulu patted Beauty's cheek. "Hi, Beauty," she said.

Beauty nodded and Lulu scratched the pretty black pony's forelock.

"Maybe when you come back from camping, there will be a new pony in my barn," said Ms. Wiggins.

"That would be so exciting," said Anna. "A baby pony."

"Actually," continued Ms. Wiggins, "I'm a little worried about Beauty. She's so small and this foal seems very large. I've decided to stay up all night with her tonight. She might need me."

Pam and Lulu exchanged a glance. Lulu knew that she and Pam had thought of the same idea at the same time. Lulu loved when that happened. Pam whispered the idea to Anna. Anna smiled and nodded.

"We have an idea," Lulu told Ms. Wiggins. "Why don't we camp here, near the barn?

Then we can take turns watching Beauty for you tonight."

"We'll wake you up if she starts to have her foal," explained Pam.

"Maybe we could all see the foal being born," added Anna.

"It would be wonderful to have some help," Ms. Wiggins said. "Are you sure you don't mind? It's not as much fun as camping in the hills."

"We'll still be sleeping in our tent," said Lulu.

"When we're not with Beauty," added Anna.

"And we might see a newborn foal," said Lulu. "That's more exciting than our regular camp-outs."

"We'll even fix up the stall for Beauty to have her baby in," said Pam. "I know just what to do."

Ms. Wiggins thanked the Pony Pals. "Now I'd better go find Mike Lacey," she said. "I want him to clean up one of the trails this afternoon."

"Good," Anna whispered to Lulu. "That means he won't be bothering us."

The Pony Pals took the saddles off their ponies, gave them some water, and led them over to Picasso's paddock. Picasso ran up and whinnied a hello to the visiting ponies.

Lulu hugged Snow White before she let her loose. "You're going to be near Beauty's little yard," she told Snow White. "She's getting ready to have her baby."

Lulu followed Pam and Anna into the barn. It was time to prepare Beauty's stall. First they cleaned out the old straw and swept the floor extra clean. Then they put in fresh straw. Pam made a big fluffy straw bed for Beauty. Lulu brought in a bucket of fresh water.

"Ponies like to be in a familiar place when they have their babies," Pam explained to Anna and Lulu. "So it's good for her to be in her stall. And it should be very quiet. We'll have to remember that when we're watching her."

Lulu went into the empty stall next to

Beauty's. "We can watch her from here," she told Anna and Pam.

"Good idea," agreed Lulu.

"We need some towels," said Pam, "to wipe off the foal when it's born."

Soon Ms. Wiggins and her caretaker, Mr. Silver, inspected Beauty's stall.

"It's perfect," Mr. Silver told them.

"Now we have to decide on turns for watching during the night," said Lulu.

"Can we write the schedule on the barn blackboard?" asked Pam.

"Certainly," answered Ms. Wiggins.

"Put me down for the six A.M. to eight A.M. shift," said Mr. Silver. "I'm doing barn chores then. I'll keep an eye on Beauty. And I'll be sure to let you know if anything starts happening."

"And I'll watch from midnight to two A.M.," said Ms. Wiggins.

The Pony Pals worked out the rest of the schedule. Pam wrote it on the blackboard in yellow chalk.

```
SCHEDULE FOR OVERNIGHT
        WATCH
10-12      PAM
12-2       MS. WIGGINS
2-4        LULU
4-6        ANNA
6-8        MR. SILVER
```

Lulu hoped that Beauty's baby would be born during the night. But mostly Lulu hoped Beauty would be okay — and that she'd have a healthy foal.

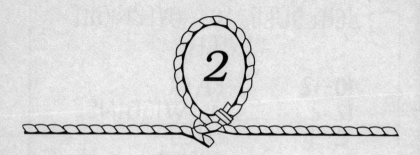

Friends

"How will we know Beauty is ready to have her baby?" asked Anna. "Does it just start being born?"

"Good question," said Lulu.

"When she's ready, Beauty will get restless," explained Pam. "She might walk in circles around the stall. Sometimes a pregnant pony will lie down and get up a lot. That's a sign, too."

"Write that all on the blackboard," suggested Anna. "So we remember."

Pam picked up the pink chalk and wrote:

SIGNS THAT A PONY IS
READY TO GIVE BIRTH

SHE IS RESTLESS & UNEASY
SHE WALKS IN CIRCLES AROUND THE STALL
SHE GETS UP AND DOWN A LOT

Pam put down the chalk. "What should we do next?" she asked.

"Let's go find a good spot for our tent," suggested Lulu.

The three friends inspected the yard between the house and the barn. Pam carried the tent, and Lulu carried the bag of stakes. They were looking for a big flat spot for their tent. No one wanted to sleep on bumpy ground.

Anna found a perfect place near the barn. The girls opened their tent and laid it out. Next they put in the tent poles. After that,

13

Lulu handed Pam the stakes and Pam pounded them in with a rock. Meanwhile, Anna kept the tent straight.

While they worked, Lulu thought about her friends. Of the three Pony Pals, Pam Crandal knew the most about ponies and horses. Her father was a veterinarian and her mother was a riding teacher. Pam had her own pony for as long as she could remember. She was an excellent rider. Pam was also the best student in their class at school. Pam loved going to school.

Anna Harley didn't like going to school as much. She was dyslexic, so reading and writing were hard for her. Even though Anna didn't like school, she worked hard. She even went to a tutor three afternoons a week. Anna was a very talented artist. She loved to draw and paint — especially ponies and horses.

Anna and Pam had lived in Wiggins all their lives. They became friends when they started kindergarten together.

Lulu didn't grow up in Wiggins. Her mother died when she was little. Her father was a naturalist who went all over the world studying wild animals and writing about them. For many years Lulu traveled with her father. But when she turned ten, Mr. Sanders said Lulu should move in with her grandmother. Mr. Sanders wanted his daughter to live in one place for a while.

Lulu thought living in Wiggins would be boring. Then she met Anna and Pam and became a Pony Pal. And then she got Snow White.

Life in Wiggins turned out to be fun and exciting. The Pony Pals were always having adventures. Tonight they might even see a foal being born.

Lulu handed the last stake to Pam. "We forgot something," Lulu told her friends.

"What?" asked Pam and Anna in unison.

"We should be watching Beauty during the day, too. Maybe she's having the foal right now and we're missing it."

15

"You're right!" exclaimed Anna.

"I'll go check on her," said Lulu. "And stay until one of you takes my place."

Lulu ran into the barn. Beauty was in the little paddock connected to her stall. Lulu went out to see her.

Beauty was standing at the fence with her head hanging over. Snow White was in the big paddock on the other side of the fence. The two ponies were sniffing faces over the fence.

Those two are such great friends, thought Lulu. I wonder if Snow White will like Beauty's foal, too.

Lulu fed carrots to Beauty, Picasso, and the other ponies. Beauty gobbled down her treat. She liked it when Lulu ran her fingers through her mane. Beauty was acting like she always did, and there were no signs that she was about to have her foal.

Soon Pam and Anna joined Lulu and the ponies.

"I'm going to ride home," Anna told Lulu. "I'll get my Walkman and some tapes. Listening to music will help us stay awake during our watch."

"Bring your tape of *Black Beauty*, too," suggested Lulu. "I love that book."

"And bring some extra snacks," added Pam.

After Anna and Acorn left, Pam and Lulu groomed their ponies. Beauty just stood in her yard and slept.

"I don't think Beauty's going to have her foal this afternoon," said Pam. "But I'll watch her just in case. You can do something else."

Snow White was full of energy from being groomed. Lulu watched her running along the fence line.

"I'll take Snow White out for a ride," Lulu told Pam. "She'd like that."

Lulu saddled up Snow White, told Pam which trail she was going on, and rode across the field. As Lulu and her pony entered the woods, Snow White whinnied happily. Lulu felt happy, too. Today was a very special day. She might see a foal being born.

After riding for fifteen minutes, Lulu noticed something on the trail ahead of them. At first, she thought it was a deer — or maybe a bear. But it wasn't either of those. It was a person. And the person was Mike Lacey.

He's cleaning up the trail for Ms. Wiggins, thought Lulu. She rode closer. Mike was dragging a fallen branch off the trail. Lulu wondered why Mike didn't look up and get out of their way. Didn't he hear them?

She rode closer and saw that Mike was wearing headphones. He *couldn't* hear them, Lulu realized.

Suddenly, Mike looked up and saw the pony and rider coming toward him. He screamed in terror.

The scream frightened Snow White and she reared up.

Mike backed away.

Lulu slipped in the saddle, but regained her balance.

"You stupid jerk!" Mike shouted at Lulu. "You almost killed me."

Lulu reined in Snow White and turned her in a circle to calm her down.

"You're the one who's stupid," Lulu told Mike. "You're not supposed to scream when you see a pony. Snow White's more afraid of you than you are of her."

Lulu turned Snow White to face the way they came.

"I'm not afraid of a dumb pony," said Mike as he backed farther away from Snow White.

"Sure you're not," said Lulu. And before Mike could say anything else, Lulu rode away on Snow White.

Mike doesn't want anyone to know he's afraid of horses and ponies, thought Lulu. But I know his big secret.

Feet First

Lulu rode Snow White up to Beauty's paddock. She couldn't wait to tell her Pony Pals about Mike. But first she had to find out about Beauty. Mr. Silver and Pam were standing at the fence, but Beauty was lying down in her stall.

"Is she going to have her foal now?" Lulu asked Mr. Silver in a whisper.

"I don't think so," answered Mr. Silver. "She's been lying like that for a while."

"Maybe she's resting up for it," said Pam.

"Could be," agreed Mr. Silver. "I'll keep an

eye on her. Why don't you girls go have your dinner?"

"Ms. Wiggins is making us spaghetti and meatballs," Pam told Lulu.

"And here comes Anna," said Lulu. "Just in time."

Anna waved to her friends as she rode across the field.

She had her Walkman, six music tapes, the tape of *Black Beauty*, and a bag of brownies. Now the Pony Pals had all the supplies they needed for their night watch.

"Guess who I saw when I was on my ride," Lulu said to her friends.

"Who?" said Anna and Pam in unison.

Lulu told them all about meeting Mike on the trail. "He was really scared of Snow White," she said. "And I don't think it was because he was surprised."

After the girls unsaddled Acorn and put him in the paddock, they walked over to Ms. Wiggins's house.

"I hope Ms. Wiggins didn't invite Mike to have dinner with us," said Pam.

"We don't have to worry about that," said Anna. "Look." She pointed to the driveway. Mike Lacey was riding his bike away from the house.

"Good riddance," said Lulu. "Let's hope he's not coming back tomorrow."

Ms. Wiggins's spaghetti dinner was delicious. The girls helped clear the table, then went back to the barn. The plan was to watch Beauty together until their separate turns began.

"Good luck," Mr. Silver told them before he left. "But don't be surprised if Beauty doesn't have her foal tonight. I don't think she's ready after all."

Lulu hoped that Mr. Silver was wrong.

The Pony Pals sat on the floor of the lookout stall. They played cards without talking and took turns standing up to check on Beauty. Beauty nibbled on hay and ignored the Pony Pals.

"She's getting used to having us around," whispered Lulu. "That's good."

At ten o'clock, Pam began her solo watch

23

and Lulu and Anna went to the tent to sleep.

Lulu stretched out her sleeping bag and zipped it up. She fell asleep wondering when Beauty's foal would be born.

"Lulu," someone whispered in her ear.

Lulu opened her eyes and saw Ms. Wiggins kneeling beside her. "It's your turn," Ms. Wiggins whispered.

Lulu unzipped her sleeping bag, pulled on her boots, and followed Ms. Wiggins out of the tent. A full moon lit up the barnyard. It was a beautiful night.

"Did anything happen yet?" Lulu asked.

"Not yet," said Ms. Wiggins. "But Beauty seems restless. Watch her carefully."

"I will," promised Lulu.

Lulu went quietly into the barn and tiptoed over to the lookout stall.

Beauty stood in the middle of her stall. Her big belly shone in the moonlight. Lulu thought she saw the foal moving around inside Beauty. Was it getting ready to come out?

Suddenly, Beauty lay down. A minute later she stood up again.

She walked in a circle around the stall.

Lulu looked at her watch. It was two-thirty.

Beauty lay down again. This time she rolled on her side and she didn't get up.

It's time, thought Lulu. The foal is ready to be born. She went to the barn phone and called Ms. Wiggins. Lulu was so excited that she almost dropped the phone.

"I'll be right there," Ms. Wiggins told Lulu. "And I'll wake up Pam and Anna on the way."

A few minutes later Ms. Wiggins and the Pony Pals were standing side by side in the lookout stall. They didn't make a sound, and they kept their eyes on Beauty.

Beauty grunted and groaned.

"She's trying to help the foal out," Ms. Wiggins whispered. "If this goes on too long, I'll call Pam's father. Beauty might need some help."

Lulu looked at her watch again. Now it was 3:15.

Beauty continued to strain and push.

When Lulu looked at her watch again, it was 3:35. "Maybe we should call Dr. Crandal now," Lulu whispered to Ms. Wiggins.

Ms. Wiggins smiled at Lulu. "I don't think we'll need Dr. Crandal after all," she said. "Look."

Lulu saw a little hoof sticking out of the opening between Beauty's legs. Then another hoof. Next, Lulu saw the foal's wet nose.

"Come on, girl," Ms. Wiggins said quietly. "You can do it."

Beauty gave a big grunt and a push, and the rest of the foal slipped out. It was all wet and sticky.

Lulu noticed tears of joy streaming down Ms. Wiggins's face.

"Good work, Beauty!" exclaimed Pam.

"That foal is so cute!" said Anna.

"Lulu, help me clean out his nostrils so he can breathe better," said Ms. Wiggins.

"I'll get Beauty some water," said Anna.

Lulu held the foal's little head, while Ms. Wiggins wiped out his nostrils. The foal gave a snort mixed with a mini-whinny sound. It was a funny noise that made them laugh. This is so wonderful, thought Lulu. We're taking care of a just-born foal.

Beauty stood up and began licking her newborn. Pam grabbed a towel and helped Beauty dry and clean the foal.

They could see that it was a male with a brown coat and black stockings.

"He's a bay like Acorn," said Anna.

"And he has a white blaze on his forehead," said Pam. "Like Lightning."

Lulu took a close look at the white marking. "It's shaped like a half-moon," she said.

It was still the middle of the night, but Lulu wasn't tired. She was interested in everything that Beauty was doing.

Beauty nuzzled and pushed the foal with her nose.

"Why is she doing that?" asked Anna.

"She wants him to get up," answered Pam.

Beauty whinnied at the foal as if to say, "Get up, you lazy kid."

They all laughed.

The foal stuck out his front legs and tried to stand. Pam put her hands under his belly and gave him a little boost. He wobbled on his skinny legs, but he was standing.

Beauty moved closer to her foal.

"Foals can't see very much the first few days," Pam explained. "Let's help him find Beauty's teat."

Lulu pushed the foal's head under Beauty's belly. He raised his little head and began to nurse.

"He's perfect," said Ms. Wiggins. "He's a perfect foal."

"Maybe I should call Mike," Ms. Wiggins said, "so he can come right over."

The Pony Pals exchanged a glance. They didn't want Mike there.

"It's four in the morning," Pam reminded Ms. Wiggins. "The phone would wake Mike's mother and sister."

"You're right," agreed Ms. Wiggins. "Mike

will be here in a few hours anyway. I know he'll be excited."

Lulu thought about Mike Lacey for a while. He was afraid of ponies. Would he *really* be excited about the foal? But soon Lulu forgot all about Mike. She had seen a foal being born, and it was the best thing she had seen in her life so far.

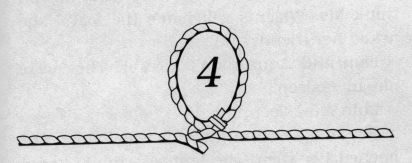

Falling

The Pony Pals and Ms. Wiggins cleaned up Beauty's stall and fed her. The foal stayed right next to his mother the whole time.

Lulu suddenly felt tired. She had only slept for a few hours.

Anna yawned.

"Maybe you girls should go back to your tent and get some sleep," suggested Ms. Wiggins.

"Okay," agreed Pam. "Let's go."

The Pony Pals went back to their tent. When they were in their sleeping bags, Lulu turned to face Anna and Pam. "What do you think Ms. Wiggins will name the foal?" she asked her friends.

Pam and Anna didn't answer. They were already asleep.

Lulu fell asleep, too.

She had a dream that she was falling. She opened her eyes. The tent was tipping over. She *was* falling!

Pam bumped into Lulu.

Lulu knocked heads with Anna.

"Ouch!" shouted Anna.

The tent was on its side. The Pony Pals, and their sleeping bags, were on top of one another.

"What happened?" asked Pam as she rolled off the pile of Pony Pals.

"Maybe it's an earthquake," said Anna as she wiggled out from under Lulu.

Lulu crawled out of her sleeping bag.

There wasn't enough space for them to stand up.

"Where's the door?" asked Anna.

"Up there," answered Pam.

Lulu looked up. The zipped flap of the tent was over her head.

"We have to tip the tent to get out," said Anna.

The girls moved around the tent until their weight tipped it upright. Lulu unzipped the flap and the three girls crawled out.

It was a sunny morning.

"How come the tent did that?" asked Anna. "It never happened before."

"There's no wind," observed Pam.

"Were the stakes in deep enough?" asked Anna.

"They were plenty deep," answered Lulu. "I saw Pam pound them in the ground myself."

"Do you think an animal could have pushed the tent over?" asked Pam. "Like a cow?"

Lulu looked around. She didn't see any cows or horses loose.

"Maybe a deer did it," suggested Anna. "A big deer. And it ran away."

"Maybe," said Lulu. "But I doubt it."

"It's a mystery," said Pam.

"Which we have to solve," added Lulu.

"But let's go see Beauty's foal first," said Anna.

"The foal!" exclaimed Lulu. "I can't wait to see him again."

Lulu crawled back into the tipped-over tent and found their boots. The girls put on their boots and ran into the barn.

"Good morning, girls," said a cheerful voice behind them.

Lulu turned around. It was Ms. Wiggins. She was carrying a big basket of muffins and containers of juice.

"I was so excited about the foal that I couldn't sleep," she said. "I made us blueberry muffins. We'll have a little celebration."

"They smell delicious," said Anna.

Beauty looked happy with her newborn. And the foal was steadier on his feet now. When he heard the girls, he moved closer to his mother.

Lulu reached over the door to pet his head. He jerked away from her.

"Don't be afraid, little foal," said Lulu. "You have to get used to people."

"Would one of you invite Mike to join us?" asked Ms. Wiggins. "He's weeding the vegetable garden."

The Pony Pals exchanged a glance. Mike Lacey was there? Did he push over their tent?

"How long has Mike been here?" asked Lulu.

"He came to work early today," said Ms. Wiggins. "He wanted to see if Beauty had her foal." Ms. Wiggins smiled. "He's very excited about the new pony."

Lulu glanced at Pam. "I'll get him," offered Lulu. "I'll pick up my camera on the way. I want to take pictures of Beauty and her foal."

Pam walked with Lulu to the barn door. "Do you think Mike tipped over our tent?" she whispered.

"I don't think he'd do it by himself," Lulu whispered back. "But it's a typical Tommy prank. Mean and dangerous. We have to get to the bottom of this."

Lulu ran over to the tent and crawled inside. Her camera had fallen out of her backpack, but it wasn't broken. Her binoculars were okay, too.

Lulu hung the camera around her neck. She put the binoculars in her pocket for safekeeping.

It was time to find Mike. She walked around to the vegetable garden. Mike wasn't there. But she did see a boy on a bicycle. He was riding away from the house.

Why is Mike leaving so soon? Lulu wondered. Is he afraid of *us*, too? She took her binoculars out and looked through them.

The boy she saw through the binoculars wasn't Mike Lacey. It was Tommy Rand. That's it, thought Lulu. If Tommy's here, I bet he *and* Mike tipped over our tent!

Then Lulu heard someone coming out of the garden shed. She quickly put her binoculars in her pocket and headed toward the noise. Mike Lacey walked out, carrying a hoe.

Lulu was mad at him because of the tent

tipping. But she decided not to let him know what she knew. It was a Pony Pal problem and the Pony Pals would decide together what to do.

"Ms. Wiggins said to come to the barn," Lulu told Mike in a calm voice. Then she turned and ran to the barn ahead of him.

When they were all in the barn, they ate the muffins and watched the foal. Mike ate two muffins in a hurry, but he didn't talk much.

When the foal came close to the gate, Mike reached over and rubbed his little nose. Maybe Mike's not afraid of the foal, thought Lulu. But he *is* afraid of grown ponies. And horses, like Picasso.

"I'd better get back to work," Mike told Ms. Wiggins.

"Wait one minute, Mike," said Ms. Wiggins. "There's something I want to talk about with you and the girls."

Does Ms. Wiggins know what Mike and Tommy did? wondered Lulu. Did she see it happen?

"It wasn't my idea," said Mike.

"No," said Ms. Wiggins. "It's my idea."

Lulu was confused. Did Ms. Wiggins help tip over the tent? It was hard to believe Ms. Wiggins would do something so dangerous.

"My idea is this," explained Ms. Wiggins. "I'd like you all to help me name Beauty's foal. Each of you should think of a name for him."

"And you'll pick your favorite?" asked Pam.

"No," said Ms. Wiggins. "The four of you will. Let's have a meeting at three o'clock on my porch. Each of you will tell us the name you've chosen and why. Then you four will vote."

Lulu liked the idea of naming the foal. But she wished Mike Lacey wasn't doing it, too.

She couldn't wait to be alone with Anna and Pam. She needed to tell them that Tommy Rand had been there.

How will we get back at the boys? wondered Lulu.

The Letter

After Mike went back to work, Lulu took pictures of the foal. There was one of him nursing while Beauty licked his back. In another, the foal was curiously sniffing Anna's hand. "I think he likes the smell of blueberry muffins," giggled Anna. Suddenly, the foal looked right at the camera. Lulu clicked another shot.

"Those are going to be adorable photos," Ms. Wiggins said.

"I'll make copies for you," Lulu told her.

As soon as Ms. Wiggins left the barn, Lulu

told Pam and Anna that she saw Tommy Rand.

"Then Mike and Tommy tipped over our tent," exclaimed Anna.

"Let's go look for evidence," suggested Lulu.

The girls went back to their campsite near the barn.

Pam found the first piece of evidence. "Look at this," she said. She held up a tent stake. "It's at least three feet from the hole."

"That means someone pulled it out and threw it," said Lulu.

Anna held up another stake. "This one wasn't near a hole, either," she said.

"Mike and Tommy took out all the stakes and then pushed the tent over," concluded Pam.

"I'm going to check for tracks," Lulu told her friends. She studied the ground all around the tent. She found a clear sneaker track in soft dirt behind the tent.

"Come see this," she called to Pam and Anna.

The three girls studied the track.

"That track is too big to be from one of our shoes," said Pam.

"It must be Tommy's or Mike's," added Anna. "Do you want me to draw it?"

"Good idea," said Lulu.

Anna took her art pad and pencil out of her backpack and made a drawing of the track.

"Mike was working in the vegetable garden before," Lulu told Anna and Pam. "I bet there are a lot of his tracks in there."

"And I bet they are identical to this track," said Anna.

"Lulu, if you do detective work in the vegetable garden," said Pam, "we'll fix the tent."

Anna handed Lulu her drawing of the track.

Lulu went around the house to the vegetable garden. Mike wasn't there anymore, so Lulu went in and walked around. She pretended that she was looking at plants. Then she found what she was *really* looking for: a clear sneaker track in the dirt between two rows of pepper plants. The track matched Anna's drawing exactly.

Lulu ran back to the campsite with her news.

"What are we going to do about those guys?" asked Anna. "They can't get away with this."

"Let's go riding," suggested Pam. "I think best when I'm riding."

"If we ride to the lake we can go for a swim," said Anna.

"And have a Pony Pal meeting about Mike and Tommy," added Lulu.

An hour later the girls and their ponies were at the edge of Lake Appamapog. The ponies rested in the shade while the girls swam.

After swimming, the three friends sat in the sun to dry off.

"So what are we going to do about Tommy and Mike?" asked Pam.

"What they did to our tent was stupid and dangerous," said Lulu. "Like all their other pranks."

Anna picked up a little stick and started a drawing in the sand. "One of us could have broken a leg or something," she said. The figure Anna drew had a cast on its leg.

"That would be awful," added Lulu. "You can't ride with a broken leg."

"Maybe we should tell Ms. Wiggins what Mike did," suggested Pam.

"Mike has a good job with Ms. Wiggins," said Lulu. "His family needs the money, so he needs the job. And Ms. Wiggins really likes him," she added.

"That's because Mike is almost a nice person when he's not with Tommy," said Anna.

"So let's not tell Ms. Wiggins," concluded Pam.

"Right," agreed Lulu. "We can deal with these guys ourselves. We don't need help."

"But we should let Mike know that *we* know they did it," said Lulu. "And that we *could* tell Ms. Wiggins."

"*And* that we know he's afraid of horses and ponies," added Pam. "What if we told people his secret?"

44

"He'd hate that," added Lulu.

"Let's write him a letter," suggested Anna.

Pam took out her notebook and the three girls worked together on the letter. When they'd finished, Lulu read it aloud.

MIKE: WE KNOW THAT YOU AND TOMMY TIPPED OVER OUR TENT. WE HAVE EVIDENCE TO PROVE IT. IF YOU DO ANYTHING MEAN AND DANGEROUS. LIKE THAT AGAIN, WE'LL TELL MS. WIGGINS. YOU BETTER LEAVE US ALONE OR YOU COULD LOSE YOUR JOB.

PAM, ANNA, LULU

P.S. WE SAW HOW AFRAID YOU WERE WHEN YOU FED PICASSO. WE WERE SPYING ON YOU.

P.P.S. WATCH OUT FOR PONY POWER!

45

"That's an excellent letter," said Anna. "Should we mail it?"

Lulu folded the letter in thirds. "I have a better idea," she said. "I'll stick it in his bicycle seat. That way he'll get it sooner."

Anna had drawn a pony in the sand. She pointed to it with her drawing stick. "We forgot something," she said. "We have to name the foal."

"Have you thought of a name?" Lulu asked Pam.

"No," answered Pam.

"Me neither," said Anna.

Lulu stood up. "Let's go back and watch him," she suggested. "Maybe that will give us ideas."

The three friends walked over to their ponies.

"We shouldn't tell one another our ideas," said Anna. "Then it will be a surprise at the naming meeting."

Lulu smiled at Anna. "Perfect," she said.

"Perfect, except Mike is going to be there," said Pam.

The girls rode back to Ms. Wiggins's barn. Pam and Anna unsaddled the three ponies while Lulu delivered Mike's mail. His bike was leaning against the garden shed. Lulu stuck the letter in the front of the bicycle seat.

Next, Lulu sneaked around the house and ran back to the paddock. Pam and Anna were leading the ponies into the paddock. Beauty and her foal were already in the yard behind the stall.

When Snow White saw Beauty she ran over to the fence. She noticed the foal, lowered her head, and nickered a friendly greeting. The foal ran back to his mother. Snow White watched every move he made.

"Snow White likes Beauty's foal," Anna told Lulu.

Lulu smiled. "Snow White loves baby ponies," she said.

"Me, too," said Anna.

Lulu studied the foal's cute little face. And it gave her an idea for a name.

Surprise Guest

The girls went over to Ms. Wiggins's porch at three o'clock. Ms. Wiggins and Mike were already there. Lulu noticed that Mike's bike was leaning against the porch. The letter from the Pony Pals was not in the seat.

"He's read our letter," Lulu whispered to Pam and Anna.

"I bet he's afraid we'll tell on him," said Anna.

Ms. Wiggins came to the porch steps to greet the girls.

Lulu poured herself some lemonade and

sat in a rocker. She looked out at the view. From Ms. Wiggins's porch, Lulu could see Picasso, Acorn, Lightning, and Snow White in the paddock.

"What did you girls do today?" asked Ms. Wiggins.

"We fixed our tent," answered Pam. She looked at Mike when she said it.

"Was it broken?" asked Ms. Wiggins.

"Not exactly," answered Anna.

Lulu noticed that Mike's face was getting red. He's really scared we'll tell, she thought.

"Our tent kind of tipped over," explained Pam.

"Maybe Mike can check it for you," said Ms. Wiggins, "so it doesn't happen again. He knows about tents." She smiled at Mike. "Didn't you camp out a lot with your dad?"

Mike shrugged his shoulders. "Yeah," he said.

Lulu remembered how Mike's father left Mrs. Lacey, Mike, and his little sister, Rosalie. Mr. Lacey moved far away and now

Mike hardly ever saw his father. Lulu felt a little sorry for Mike. But only just a little.

"Hey," a boy's voice shouted.

Lulu turned around and saw Tommy Rand jumping off his bike.

Tommy came up the porch steps two at a time.

"What are *you* doing here?" blurted out Pam.

"He came to meet me," Mike mumbled.

"What's up?" asked Tommy. He grinned at Mike. "A tea party?"

"Why don't you sit down and have a snack with us, Tommy?" said Ms. Wiggins. "We're having a little contest for naming the new foal. The one you saw this morning. Everyone tells a name and says why it's a good name for Beauty's foal."

"Okay," said Tommy. "I'll play."

He sat on the porch railing and grinned around at the Pony Pals. That's the Tommy grin that spells trouble, thought Lulu. She glared at him.

51

"I'll get a glass for Tommy's lemonade," said Ms. Wiggins. "When I come back we'll have the contest."

As soon as Ms. Wiggins was gone, Tommy hit his knee and laughed. "A contest to name the little pony," he said in a teasing voice. "Man, I have a great idea."

"What?" said Mike.

What stupid idea will he have? Lulu wondered.

Tommy looked around at the Pony Pals and Mike. "Here's what we do," he said. "We all come up with a really crazy name. Like, I'm going to say, *I think you should name the foal Turd. I chose that name because of his color.*"

"But . . ." Mike began.

"You don't think it's a funny idea, Mike?" asked Tommy. "You *afraid* of Ms. Wiggins?"

"Tommy Rand, you are so *dumb*," said Pam. "You should just leave now."

"You're nothing but trouble," hissed Anna.

"And your idea is *mean*," added Lulu. "Ms.

Wiggins is our friend. And you're making fun of her idea."

"It's a *joke*," said Tommy. "The Pony Pests have no sense of humor."

"Not when people are doing stupid, mean, dangerous things," said Lulu.

"Like tipping over tents!" added Pam.

Tommy laughed harder than ever.

Just then Ms. Wiggins came out with the snacks. She handed Tommy a glass of lemonade. "I'm glad you're having such a good time, Tommy," she said.

Lulu and Pam exchanged a glance. Didn't Ms. Wiggins know that Tommy was a troublemaker?

Ms. Wiggins sat back down in her rocker. "So, Pam, what's your idea for a name?" asked Ms. Wiggins.

"I think you should call him *Rascal*," said Pam. "His eyes already sparkle with mischief."

While Pam was talking, Tommy mimicked her. Ms. Wiggins couldn't see him. But the Pony Pals could.

"Rascal is a cute name," said Ms. Wiggins. "How about you, Lulu? What's your idea?"

"Let Mike go next," said Tommy. He winked at Mike when he said it.

"All right," agreed Ms. Wiggins. "What's your idea, Mike?"

Lulu held her breath. What would Mike do? Would he give a real name for the foal? Or would he make fun of Ms. Wiggins's idea, to please Tommy?

Just then, Snow White made a shrill, loud whinny. Lulu recognized that sound. It meant that Snow White was upset about something. Lulu looked out to the paddock. Snow White was standing at the fence separating the paddock from Beauty and the foal's yard.

Snow White was telling her something was wrong. What could it be?

Barn Call

Snow White whinnied again.

"Something's wrong in Beauty's yard," Lulu told Ms. Wiggins and her Pony Pals.

She jumped over the porch railing and ran toward the paddock.

"I'm coming," Lulu shouted to her pony.

Ms. Wiggins, Pam, and Anna followed Lulu.

Lulu climbed through the fence rails. "What's wrong, Snow White?" she asked.

Snow White nodded toward Beauty's little paddock.

Beauty was just standing there. The foal sat next to her. That's not unusual, thought Lulu. Foals lie down a lot. She looked around. There were no other animals in the yard to cause trouble.

Had a fox been in the yard? wondered Lulu. Or a stray dog? Is that what upset Snow White?

Lulu went through the gate and walked up to the foal. "Are you okay?" she asked as she leaned over him.

The foal's breath came out in little wheezy sounds.

Ms. Wiggins, Pam, and Anna were in the yard now, too. Mike and Tommy stayed on the paddock side of the fence.

"He's breathing funny," Lulu told them.

The foal coughed.

"It sounds bad," said Mike.

Ms. Wiggins and Pam knelt down beside the foal. Pam put her head on his chest. "He's congested," she reported to the others.

"I'm going to call Dr. Crandal," Ms. Wiggins said as she headed into the barn.

As soon as Ms. Wiggins was gone, Tommy Rand spoke up. "Has the little pony got a little cold-y?" he asked in a silly voice.

"Quit it, Tommy," Mike mumbled. "This could be serious."

Lulu turned to Tommy. "Not everything is a joke, Tommy Rand," she said.

"Well, the Pony Pests are one big joke," said Tommy. "You make me laugh all day long."

"And *you* make me sick," Pam told Tommy. "Don't you take anything seriously?"

Lulu put a hand on Pam's arm. This wasn't the time to have a fight with Tommy Rand.

Mike looked from Tommy to the Pony Pals. "Let's go, man," he said.

"Yeah, man," agreed Tommy. "We got better stuff to do."

As the two boys walked away, Mike looked over his shoulder at the foal. Mike doesn't want to leave, thought Lulu.

Lulu turned her attention back to the foal.

Beauty was nudging him with her nose. But he didn't get up.

Ms. Wiggins came back to the yard. "I reached Dr. Crandal on his cell phone," she said. "He's on a barn call. He'll be here in a few minutes."

Snow White hung her head over the fence and nickered gently.

"Snow White's worried about the foal, too," said Anna.

"I'm afraid our darling foal has pneumonia," said Ms. Wiggins. "It happens with newborns sometimes. It can be very dangerous in such a young one."

"Poor baby," said Anna.

"Let's clean out Beauty's stall and put in fresh straw," suggested Pam.

"Thank you, girls," said Ms. Wiggins. "Thank you for all your help." She sounded very worried.

By the time the girls had fixed up the stall, Dr. Crandal had arrived.

He listened to the foal's breathing with a

stethoscope and looked in his eyes and mouth. Next, he took the foal's temperature and felt his joints.

"It's pneumonia, all right," said Dr. Crandal. "The first thing we should do is bring Beauty and this little fellow inside."

Dr. Crandal carried the foal into the stall. Beauty followed them.

Lulu went over to Snow White. "Sorry, Snow White," she said. "You can't see Beauty and her baby for a while." She patted Snow White's cheek and gave her a kiss.

Lulu joined Pam and Anna in the empty stall next to Beauty's.

Dr. Crandal took a needle out of his doctor's bag. "This is an antibiotic," he explained. He gave the foal a shot in the rump.

Anna winced. Lulu knew that Anna hated getting shots and seeing other people get them. But it didn't bother her and Pam that much.

Dr. Crandal took out another needle. "This shot is to bring down his fever," he said.

"Dad, what can we do to take care of him?" asked Pam.

"Keep him warm and make sure he nurses," answered Dr. Crandal. "It's important for him to have plenty of fluids. He's a very sick foal right now, so watch him carefully."

Pam took out her notebook and wrote down her father's instructions.

"I'll come by in the morning to check on him," he added. "If there's a change for the worse during the night, call me."

After Dr. Crandal left, Ms. Wiggins looked at her pony and the foal and sighed. "We'll have to keep a good watch over this foal," she said.

"We'll help," said Lulu and Anna in unison.

"We can watch him tonight," added Pam. "We'll sleep over again."

Ms. Wiggins looked around at the Pony Pals. "That would be very helpful," she said.

"If we went home we'd just worry about him the whole time," said Pam.

The little pony coughed again.

Beauty nickered as if to say, "What's wrong with my baby?"

Lulu stroked Beauty's head. "It'll be okay," she said. "We'll take care of him."

Ms. Wiggins sighed. "Beauty has had a hard life," she said. "I hope nothing happens to her foal."

Lulu nodded in agreement. She remembered when they found Beauty alone and starving in a field. The Pony Pals and Ms. Wiggins had saved Beauty's life.

Lulu hoped that now they could save her foal's life, too.

Where's Tommy?

The Pony Pals and Ms. Wiggins went over to the blackboard. Anna erased the schedule and list from the day before.

"Beauty's baby isn't even one day old," said Anna.

"He's very young to be so sick," added Pam.

Lulu heard someone come into the barn. It was Mike Lacey. Ms. Wiggins met him at Beauty's stall. The Pony Pals stayed by the blackboard.

"Mike," said Ms. Wiggins. "I wondered where you'd gone to. Where's Tommy?"

"Someplace making trouble," Pam whispered to Lulu.

"Tommy — ah — had to go," Mike told Ms. Wiggins. "I — ah — went for a ride with him."

So Mike left to get rid of Tommy, thought Lulu.

"How's the foal?" asked Mike. "Is he going to be okay?"

Ms. Wiggins told Mike everything that Dr. Crandal had said. "The Pony Pals and I are going to watch him tonight," she added.

"I'll do that, too," offered Mike. "I want to help."

"Oh, no," Pam groaned in Lulu's ear.

"Thank you, Mike," said Ms. Wiggins. "If you take a turn, the girls can have shorter shifts. That would be a big help. They didn't have much sleep last night."

"Because *he* tipped over our tent," Lulu whispered to Anna.

Ms. Wiggins and Mike joined the Pony Pals at the blackboard. It was time to figure out a schedule. Mike didn't look at the Pony Pals, and they didn't look at him. Ms. Wiggins might like him, thought Lulu. But I don't.

```
SCHEDULE FOR OVERNIGHT
         WATCH
  10 - 11:30        ANNA
  11:30 - 1:30      MS. WIGGINS
  1:30 - 3:00       LULU
  3:00 - 4:30       MIKE
  4:30 - 6:00       PAM
  6:00 - 8:00       MR. SILVER
```

When the schedule was done, the girls went back to their campsite. Mike stayed to watch the foal.

"Let's air our sleeping bags," suggested Pam.

The girls took their bags out of the tent, unzipped them, and laid them out on the lawn.

"I'm really worried about the foal," said Anna.

"He could die from pneumonia," added Lulu. "We have to watch him very carefully."

"Do you think Mike knows how to watch him?" asked Anna.

"He doesn't know very much about ponies," said Pam.

"And he's afraid of them," added Lulu.

"We'd better talk to him," said Pam.

"Let's go find him," suggested Lulu.

The girls went into the barn. Mike was leaning on the door to Beauty's stall and watching the foal. "How is he?" asked Lulu.

"I don't think he's breathing right," said Mike.

Pam went into the stall and put her ear to the foal's chest. "He's the same as before," she reported to Mike and her Pony Pals.

Lulu felt the foal's neck. "He's still warm," she reported, "but he's not any hotter than he was."

"He should nurse a lot," Anna told Mike. "He needs lots of fluids."

"And check to see if he's hot," instructed Lulu. "That means his fever is up."

"You have to go into the stall with him and Beauty to check him," added Anna. "Are you sure you can do that?"

" 'Course I can," answered Mike with a scowl.

"If you think he's getting sicker during your watch tonight, Mike," said Pam, "go for help."

"There could be an emergency during the night," Lulu told Mike.

"Okay, okay," said Mike impatiently. "I got it. I'm not stupid."

The Pony Pals just looked at him.

"Sometimes you are," said Pam. "When you follow whatever *stupid, dumb, dangerous* thing Tommy Rand says."

"You're even *afraid* of Tommy. And we know you're afraid of ponies, too," added Lulu.

"Pony Pests," muttered Mike. He turned around and left the barn. The barn door banged behind him.

Just then the foal coughed. "I'll watch him for a while," Pam told Anna and Lulu.

"We'll check on our ponies," said Anna.

Anna and Lulu went out to the paddock. Lightning and Acorn came over to the girls. Snow White didn't pay any attention. She was still staying close to Beauty's paddock.

"Snow White is worried about the foal, too," said Lulu. She went over to her pony. "There's nothing you can do for him, Snow White. We'll take good care of him."

But will Mike? Lulu wondered.

Night Watch

Lulu opened her eyes in the dark tent. Someone was whispering her name. It was Ms. Wiggins.

"It's your turn to watch, Lulu," she whispered.

Lulu unzipped her sleeping bag, pulled on her boots, and went outside. "How's the foal?" asked Lulu.

"He nursed and now he's sleeping," said Ms. Wiggins. "It's very peaceful in the barn."

"Do I have to wake Mike up for his turn?" asked Lulu.

"No," answered Ms. Wiggins. "There's an alarm clock in the guest room. I set it for two-forty-five."

Lulu walked quietly into the barn. Beauty was sleeping standing up and the foal was curled up on the straw. His breathing was noisy, but steady.

Lulu went into the lookout stall. She opened an apple juice, took three cookies, and sat on the stool. From the stool she could see everything that went on in Beauty's stall.

Beauty and her foal slept all during Lulu's watch. Lulu yawned a lot. It was hard to stay awake.

At three o'clock Mike came into the barn to take Lulu's place. He looked sleepy, too.

"How's it going?" he asked.

"Nothing's happened," answered Lulu. "They're just sleeping."

"Does that mean the foal's getting better?" asked Mike.

Lulu slid off the stool. "I guess," she said. "But he's still breathing a little funny."

"Okay," Mike said. "You can go."

I don't trust Mike Lacey, thought Lulu as she walked back to the tent. She looked around. He and Tommy could be getting ready to play another trick. And Mike is afraid of ponies to begin with.

A few minutes later, Lulu was curled up in her sleeping bag, sound asleep.

She woke up with a start. The tent was shaking.

"It's them again!" shouted Pam.

"You *creeps*!" screamed Anna.

Pam unzipped the tent flap. Mike was standing there.

The three girls pushed past him to get out of the tent.

"What are you doing here?" Lulu asked Mike.

"You're supposed to be watching the foal," shouted Anna.

"Where's Tommy?" asked Lulu.

"Something's wrong with the foal," said Mike. "He's acting weird and coughing and . . ."

73

Lulu didn't hear the rest of what Mike said. She was already running into the barn.

Pam, Anna, and Mike came in behind her.

The foal was coughing and trying to get up. Beauty whinnied as if to say, "Somebody help my baby!"

Pam went into the stall and put her hands under the foal's belly. She lifted to help him stand. The foal heaved a sigh and started breathing more smoothly.

"He's not hot anymore," Pam told the others. "I think his fever is down."

"Maybe he should nurse now," suggested Anna.

Just then the foal moved under his mother, raised his head, and began to nurse.

"But he was coughing over and over," said Mike. "Isn't that bad?"

"He's all right now," said Pam. She looked at her watch. "It's time for my turn. You can go, Mike."

Mike rubbed Beauty's neck. " 'Night, Beauty," he whispered.

Mike left.

"It's a good thing Mike got us," said Pam. "For once he did the right thing. He didn't even seem afraid of the foal."

"Maybe he was afraid of being alone in the barn, though," said Lulu.

"Maybe Mike and Tommy are messing with our tent right now," added Anna.

"You and Lulu go check," said Pam. "I'll stay here with the foal."

"What if the boys play a trick on you, Pam?" whispered Anna. "You're all alone."

Pam patted her pocket. "I have my whistle. If I need help, I'll let you know."

Anna and Lulu went back to the tent. They carefully checked it over — inside and out. No one had disturbed a thing.

Lulu didn't feel sleepy anymore. "You go back to sleep," she told Anna. "I'm going to stay up and watch the sunrise."

Anna yawned. "Okay," she said. "Wake me up if you need help."

Lulu sat under a tree near the tent. She remembered when she had pneumonia. She had coughed a lot. Especially when she got up after lying down. That's what happened to the foal, thought Lulu.

Lulu looked up and saw a white shape running through the dawning light.

It was Snow White.

Soon the sun would rise and a new day would begin. Lulu wondered what that day would bring.

The Name Game

Lulu was still sitting outside the tent when Pam came back from her watch. "Any sign of Mike or Tommy?" asked Pam.

"No," answered Lulu. "It's been very quiet. Anna went back to sleep."

Ms. Wiggins passed them on her way to the barn. "Good morning, girls," she said. "How's the foal doing?"

"He seems better," answered Pam. "He was nursing when I left. Mr. Silver is there now."

"There's breakfast for you girls in the

house," said Ms. Wiggins. "I'll wait in the barn for Dr. Crandal."

Anna stuck her head out of the opened tent flap. "Breakfast?" she said in a sleepy voice. They all laughed.

The three girls went to the house to clean up and have breakfast.

When Lulu came out of the bathroom, Anna was waiting her turn. "Mike's in the kitchen," Anna warned Lulu.

Lulu walked into the kitchen and looked around. Pam was making toast at the counter. Mike sat at the big kitchen table. He was wolfing down a bowl of cereal. Lulu poured cereal for herself and sat down, too. Mike passed her the milk.

"Thanks," she said.

No one said anything for a while. Finally, Mike mumbled something Lulu couldn't understand.

"What?" she asked.

"Sorry I scared you guys last night," he said a little louder. Then he got up and left the room.

Pam and Lulu exchanged a glance. They were both surprised that Mike had apologized.

Lulu put her dirty cereal bowl in the sink. Through the window she saw a car come up the driveway. "It's your dad," she told Pam.

The Pony Pals and Mike went back to the barn. They watched Dr. Crandal examine the foal.

"He's definitely getting better," said Dr. Crandal. "No one needs to stay up with him tonight. Just check on him a few times during the day. I'll give him another antibiotic shot."

"Can he go outside today?" asked Lulu.

"Yes," Dr. Crandal answered. "Since the weather is so nice. But if it turns bad, bring him in again. And definitely keep him in at night."

Dr. Crandal put his equipment back in his bag. "What is this little fellow's name, anyway?" he asked as he left the stall.

"We haven't decided yet," answered Ms. Wiggins. "We're working on it."

"Well, let me know when he has a name,"

Dr. Crandal said. "I want to put it in my records." He rubbed the little half-moon marking on the foal's forelock. "He's my newest patient."

Dr. Crandal said good-bye to everyone and left.

Ms. Wiggins smiled around at the Pony Pals and Mike. "Thank you all for taking such good care of Beauty's foal. Let's meet on the porch in two hours and *finally* name Dr. Crandal's newest patient."

"Can we do it right now?" asked Lulu. "We already have ideas."

"But Tommy had an idea for a name, too," said Ms. Wiggins. "We have to give him time to get here. Mike can phone him or go on his bike and find him."

Lulu and Pam exchanged a glance. How could they keep Tommy Rand from ruining the naming game?

"Tommy's really busy today," Mike told Ms. Wiggins. "He can't come."

Mike doesn't want Tommy here, either, thought Lulu.

"Besides, Tommy didn't have any good ideas," added Anna. "He was just fooling around."

"He was acting real silly about the whole thing," said Lulu.

Mike didn't say anything, but he nodded.

Pam erased the blackboard. "We can write the names here," she suggested. "Then vote."

"All right," agreed Ms. Wiggins. "If that's what you all want."

"It is," the Pony Pals said in unison. Mike smiled.

"Pam, you already told us your idea," said Lulu. "Did you change your mind?"

"No," said Pam as she picked up a piece of chalk. "I still like Rascal." She wrote RASCAL on the board.

"I'll go next," offered Lulu.

She took the chalk from Mike and wrote MOON on the board. "The foal has a half-moon marking on his forehead," explained Lulu. "And there was a full moon the night he was born."

Anna took the chalk from Lulu and wrote

BIG BOY. "I had that idea because he was such a big foal," said Anna. She smiled at Lulu. "I like your idea better."

"Big Boy's a cute name," said Pam. "Then we could call him B.B."

Anna wrote B.B. in parentheses next to Big Boy.

"That just leaves you, Mike," said Ms. Wiggins.

Mike took the chalk from Anna and carefully printed MIRACLE on the board.

"That's my name for him," Mike said quietly.

"Why?" asked Anna. "You're supposed to say why."

"Because," Mike continued, "it's like a miracle that he was born without any problems. Then he got sick, and it's a miracle he didn't die."

Mike looked at the floor the whole time he was talking. Mike Lacey is very shy, thought Lulu.

"So that's all the names," said Ms. Wiggins. "How do you want to vote?"

"Let's do a secret ballot," suggested Pam.

"That's good," said Anna.

Lulu and Mike agreed to the secret ballot, too.

Pam took four pieces of paper from her notebook. She had two pencils for them to share.

Lulu studied the list on the board.

RASCAL

MOON

BIG BOY (B.B.)

MIRACLE

Which one was the best name for the foal? She thought about the last forty-eight hours. They'd watched the foal be born. He became very sick the first day of his life, but he survived. Lulu knew that there was only one name for him.

She wrote down her choice, folded her ballot, and handed it to Ms. Wiggins.

When all the votes were in, Ms. Wiggins mixed them up and opened one.

"We have a vote for Moon," Ms. Wiggins announced.

Pam wrote "1" next to the name Moon. Lulu wondered who voted for her idea.

Ms. Wiggins opened the next ballot. "Here's a vote for Miracle," she said.

Pam made a "1" next to Miracle.

Ms. Wiggins opened the third ballot. "Another vote for Miracle," she said.

Pam erased the "1" next to Miracle and wrote "2."

"And," said Ms. Wiggins, opening the last ballot. "*Another* vote for Miracle." Ms. Wiggins smiled at Mike. "Miracle is a wonderful name for the new foal, Mike. Thank you."

Mike looked surprised.

The Pony Pals looked at one another. They all liked the foal's name.

"It's a perfect name for him," Lulu told Mike.

"Ah, yeah, thanks," mumbled Mike.

"Thank you all," said Ms. Wiggins. "Come over to the house, and I'll make you a nice big lunch."

"Lunch!" exclaimed Pam. "We forgot to feed our ponies."

"Then we'll come over to the house," Lulu told Ms. Wiggins.

The Pony Pals went to the other end of the barn for grain.

Lulu held up a bucket and Pam scooped in grain.

"Who voted for my idea?" Lulu asked.

"Not me," said Pam. "I voted for Miracle."

"Me, too," said Anna.

"So Mike voted for your idea, Lulu," said Anna.

"I guess he liked Moon better than Miracle," said Lulu.

"I'm going to draw a picture of Miracle today," said Anna.

The girls took the buckets of grain to their

ponies. The ponies ran to the fence to meet them. Snow White whinnied as if to say, "It's about time!"

Lulu put the bucket of food down for her pony. She stood beside Snow White while she ate. "Snow White," she said. "You told us the foal was sick. Now he's better and his name is Miracle."

Across the paddock, Lulu saw Beauty and Miracle going into their little paddock. Snow White noticed them, too. She nickered, as if to say, "Where've you two been?"

Lulu laughed. "You're great, Snow White," she told her pony. "*You* are the miracle in my life."

Dear Reader,

I am having fun researching and writing the Pony Pal books. I've met great kids and wonderful ponies at homes, farms, and riding schools. Some of my ideas for Pony Pal adventures have even come from these visits!

I remember the day I made up the main characters for the series. I was walking on a country road in New England. First, I decided that the three girls would be smart, independent, and kind. Then I gave them their names—Pam, Anna, and Lulu. (Look at the initial of each girl's name. See what it spells when you put them together!) Later, I created the three ponies. When I reached home, I turned on my computer and started to write. And I haven't stopped since!

My friends say that I am a little bit like all of the Pony Pals. I am very organized, like Pam. I love nature, like Lulu. But I think that I am most like Anna. I am dyslexic and a good artist, just like her.

Readers often wonder about my life. I live in an apartment in New York City near Central Park and the Museum of Natural History. I enjoy swimming, hiking, painting, and reading. I also love to make up stories. I have been writing novels for children and young adults for more than twenty years! Several of my books have won the Children's Choice Award.

Many Pony Pal readers send me letters, drawings, and photos. I tape them to the wall in my office. They inspire me to write more Pony Pal stories. Thank you very much!

I don't ride anymore and I've never had a pony. But you don't have to ride to love ponies! And you certainly don't need a pony to be a Pony Pal.

Happy Reading,

Jeanne Betancourt